Weird guests

FAHRUDIN KUČUK

Globland Books

FAHRUDIN KUČUK

Weird guests

On the planet Tetran

Planet Tetran, 5981. The Ruler of the planet, powerful Dem, was standing bent over the galactic screen with just one thought: "How to save people from the future danger? Why is this happening to me? Is there a solution? There must be one!" He lifted his hand and turned his palm: "Call me professor Kazom!" The pale blue light came out of nowhere: "You called for me powerful Dem! My mind is at Your service." Dem turned to him angrily: "Hmmm, your mind! Your mind put us into one hopeless situation! What will you make up now?!", he asked him angrily trembling from anguish. Kazam started to sweat. He was thin and tall but he was shaking with fear like a dry leaf on the wind. "Do with me whatever you like, but we do not have another option. We have to leave the planet." Then they heard the voice from a teleport deck: "I am asking for the reception of two passengers from the planet Zorg." Dem jumped in front of the Kazam and took his neck and shook very strongly. " Damn you, you invited them, nothing is important to you! Not even the fact that we are going to lose something that we were making for thou-sands of years, and the heritage of our fami-lies. You have sold us! You have sold us all, do you understand?!" The light shine started to form two faces, they have looked like one egg to another, with huge hips and even bigger heads with staring eyes that were looking exactly at Dem. This one who was closer to Dem, he was a little bigger and he bent and said proudly: "My name is Artav." The other one said: "My name is Olz. We came to see if you will accept our conditions?" "Conditions, you say? Well, these were no conditions, this was the ultimatum! All of this happened because of this fool!", Dem said angrily and turned his head to Kazom.

"Ha, ha, ha", they laughed ironically. "You are naïve Dem, like the desert that is expecting for a rain, you are searching for a solution and you know very well that there is no one. You better listen to my suggestion", Artav said.

„«The suggestion!? I do not want to hear anything from you. You have forgotten about the promise that you gave to my father who raised you as well as me! You got everything from him: knowledge, power, fortune…

Now you are leaving all that for nothing I should have known, Artav.", Dem said in a disappointment. Artav came closer to Dem and yelled in his face: "I have never forgiven you our mutual childhood, you were better at everything, and our father, Big Rabod always loved you more than me!!!" They were standing there one to another, looking at each other without words. The strong brain waves were crushing trying to overpower one to the other. The strength of vibrations made a picture of planet fights, destroyed civilizations and cultures, nature that is dying, and after that came a total darkness. Dem took his head, fell on knees from the strength of a hit. He screamed from terrible pains rolling down on the nice hall. Artav stood bent trying to hold his knees with hands. He was seriously exhausted, so he turned to Olz: "Quickly, give me some pyramidal crystals." Olz came to Artav and put the crystals in his hands. Artav suddenly stopped bending and screaming, he stood on his knees and hold his hands with crystals turned to Dem. "Kill me once. What are you waiting for?!", he turned to Artav pleadingly. "You are seeking for an end too fast! No, you will not die in that way. I have prepared one nice game just for you, you will see. I think that you will like it." In just two steps, he came in front of the galactic screen, and with the speed of a light, he put his hands inside of it and quickly pulled it out. He was holding a black shadow, he shook her and in one moment nothing could be seen in the hall. Suddenly, the whole hall shined. In front of their eyes they could see the whole Solar System. Planets that surrounded the Sun slowly moved around it in one calming rhythm. "You see Dem, this is your choice. This Solar System was invented by Your father Big Rabod, and there is your end. You will be banished there if you manage to find it. If you got lucky, you may survive. Maybe you find your father alive, too. Ha, ha, ha!" he laughed like the crazy one. "I will give you pyramidal crystals that will give you twenty years of flight with two ships, this is more than enough to find Solar System", Olz said. Dem understood it was clear and that he did not have a chance to say anything else. He turned his back and came to the exit of the hall. Suddenly, like he had thought of something important he turned around and said: "You are making a big mistake, Artav! I will find that planet and make developed civilization when I become ready I will come back and destroy you! Do you hear me? You should not leave me in life!", Dem threatened and left the hall. Olz and Artav looked at each other in dibelief. Their look like said that letting Dem go was the biggest mistake in their lives. The traitor Kazom came and rubbed his hands: "What have I told you? I knew that you could get rid of him easily! Now we can fulfill our plan…So, I will become a ruler of the planet in your name and for a prize I will get all the gold of this galaxy." While he was thinking about the gold that was waiting for him, he started to squirm with pleasure looking like the hungry wolf that was looking at his prey. Artav patted his head and said: "Of course Kazom, of course everything will be as we said." He turned to Olz and gave a sign with his head. Olz invited Kazom: "Came here so that I can give You what I have promised." Kazom came quickly with great expectations. Suddenly there appeared a glass bowl: "Put this on the head he said." Kazom did as they ask because he was thinking about his enormous greed. Behind his back there was Artav who was waiting for him and squeezed his neck so tightly. Kazom could not even blink and his brain was already soaked in the bowl. "Pour in the liquid for the brain freshness but be very careful that someone does not touch him with hand. He could again transform and we could not trick him anymore." Artav ordered to Olz. Artav brought the rest of Kazams body that was crumpled like a rag. He threw it into the galactic ocean and it disappeared in one moment. That was all observed by Olz and he felt sorry for Kazom so he shook and wanted to go somewhere else and he asked: "Should I go outside to control everything and to see if they respect your decisions, Artav?" "Big Artav! That is my name from now on, is it clear?! Even your life is in my hands! And now you can go" he finished pointing at the door. Artav started to walk over the hall spreading his arms towards the stars and sang happily:

"I am returning my debt my darkness lord
I rely on your shoulder that is enough I can afford
Two rulers I banished on the place cold
That is the vow old.
When the wind started to blow nice
Every life will be transformed in ice.
They will turned off the lights
Darkness without fights
For your reign it will be a sign
It was for you a present of mine.

He finished his song and he came closer to the screen. "I, the big Artav, pronounce myself to the ruler of galaxy. R.S.N.P.- 2007!" He came closer and touched the screen with his hands. Soon some pictures of his followers started to appear on the screen, and they confirmed his rules. The flight through a galaxy showed a picture of neat work and technology. In two rows one could see enormous pyramids made from pure crystal where one could see blue thunders from up till down. Soon two ships came and they were slowly passing towards the pyramids. On the first two pyramids the tops were so shiny and hot that was the sign that the ships could landed. Two ships made from the pure gold were put exactly over the tops of pyramids that were pre-pared for landing. Soon those ships touched the pyramids and calmed it down. One could hear the voice from nowhere: "It is time for a flight, 30 minutes, so please passengers come in."

From the castle of a ruler there were rows of flying platforms that brought six coffins in the shape of human body. Coffins were actually beds for the passengers of these two ships. They looked miraculously. They were made from the pure gold. The whole beds were written in the letters of the planet Tetran- the symbolic signs that told us about the ances-try and status of passengers. Artav observed it carefully from its commanding tower, because he wanted something unexpected to hap-pen. Platforms slowly entered the lower part of pyramids, the thunder started to move. It lasted for only one moment and then coffins disappeared in ships. There was a short shine and the ships disappeared, too. Artav sighed and called for Olz. This one came quickly: "You called for me, master, Big Artav?", said

slowly bending down to the ground.

"Listen carefully what I will say. Bring me what is left from Kazom, I have one strange feeling about him. We need to destroy him forever." This one was in the main room al-ready, he tried to search for a glass bowl with the content that was left from Kazom. He fell in panic because he did not see it anywhere and he started to talk with himself in fear: "It is not possible that it was gone. Oh, Lord what can I do! Artav will not like this, he will immediately say that I it was my fault. ", he was looking all around but he could not find it and he knew that he must find a solution. Suddenly he heard tough breathing behind himself, he turned around and saw his father Žal, who told him with a fathers voice: "My son, I can see that you succeeded in life. You are the first one next to the Artav so you have completely   forgotten on your father",

he came closer to Olz. Olz got the idea. He smiled wisely: "Come my father, let me hug you. How could I forget on you?!" His father fell into his arms and Olz did the exact thing that Arkad did to Kazom. The brain of his father fell into the glass jar immediately. "Arkad will not know that I have tricked him. I am a pure genius. "Are you coming?", Artav yelled threatening. Olz was already near him and gave him the jar. He took it and brought it closer to his head and said: "What will we do now Kazom? Your real master left you, so what can I do?", he finished the question laughing at the jar.

"No, no master. Do not ask him anything because he is very wise so he could find the solution to trick us!", in the fear said Olz. He turned to Olz and looked in his eyes. It lasted for a few moments and he started to laugh: "Once in life you said the proper thing! I can not imagine that you have start thinking. Well done! But do not make it like a common thing." He put the bowl on the table and asked from Olz to bring him some white worms. "My biggest mind, your time passed by", he poured the brain content into a bowl. The whole content was quickly eaten by worms.

A Journey

Ships were flying in pairs on a huge place and without small speed, bringing their passengers into the unknown. The inner part of the ship did not release anything about the type of trip. Passengers did not show any signs of life while they were laying in the golden coffins. Only one of the present people was awake- Kazom, or better to say what was left from him. The glass bowl with his brain. He managed to trick Artav and came on the ship on only way that was known well to him. It was only left to try transformation into any shape that would give him a possibility into a farther action.

The brain started to pulse mixing the liquid, first slowly then faster and faster. From the strenght of mixing a water leech was made and it started to push a brain outside the bowl. The leech, together with the brain, flew out and started to float in the air seeking for on object where she could be placed. Kazom saw one concept- the board where was usually picture and numerous information. He came closer to it looking for the entrance - the programmer card. Very soon he found it under one navigator and decided in one second. All gray mass in one moment was pulled in the thickness of the entrance and very soon disappeared in it. The inner part of the key ship system looked like the town in small. Different chips were put in small rows and numbers looked like streets and buildings, they only missed citizens. When Kazom entered the system, electronic town got one new life. Like the sunshine, Kazoms brain soaked the whole device and took all the energy and data that were held in him. All information were gathered in one device. Kazom asked information about the planet where they were going on, the part of life, as well as the development of civilization.

He gained feedback that was supported by the picture and speech. "Around Solar system there are nine planets. The planet that we are travelling to has population similar to us but they are still on a primitive level of revolution." By listening to these data, in front of the Kazom there were creatures of Blue Planet. Kazom looked carefully at the unknown creature. The picture was viral and Kazom gained the complete insight in that character. The elementary data came outside, the height, weight and age. Data was a real thrill to Kazom so decided to take an offered shape.

He turned on a program with transformation data and he stood under the glass bell in the lower part of the ship. He heard slow music and he gained magical green color. Music was louder and the green color danced faster with the vibration of a bell. Kazamas brain accepted a strange dance and moved up and down. In one moment the bell was covered in darkness, nothing could be recognized, the music was lowered and it became sad and tired. The cry of one child was there and then it became like a disappointment.

Darkness was exchanged for a light. Light means birth- a new life. Kazom moved light and came out sobbing. Only his head was the same as before, the head of one young and beautiful man, the rest of the body looked like some other shape of life that was unknown to him. He made a first move, and fell. He was thinking while he was laying why he can not walk. Any doubt disappeared when he figured out that all four limbs are supposed to be used for a walk. He tried again now, he was more stable this time. He felt like he was on ice, the enormous energy was spread in his body. He gained the wish to jump. He jumped immediately. The jump was moved with a huge strenght. He felt like a beast full of force and energy so he jumped over on the other part of the room. He gained date: "You passed 350.954 kilometers. Till the end of the road there is still 20.056 kilometers. The purpose is- the planet Disappearance."

" What does this mean?", he screamed angrily. He was in a search for a solution. He knew he did not have a lot of time. His brain worked with enormous speed. He tried to change with his paw a program. He did not succeed because the enormous paw pushed more orders, so the central memory could not resist and tried to seek for a solution. He knew he

did not have a lot of time. His brain was working with an enormous speed. He tried to change programs with his paws. He did not succeed because the enormous paw hid many commands so the central data could not find out what was the real instruction. He lifted his hands to his face and saw slits on them. He tried with his whole panic, fear and battle for life towards paws and suddenly saw clutches.

The strong and shiny clutches like swords, and Kazom entered the coordinates in order to turn the ship to the other direction. On the screen he saw that time was ticking. "Till the end of the road only 20 seconds was left."

Kazom's clutches flew like a thunder on the screen. He was left with only five seconds. When he pressed the command, he gained the confirmation about reception.

Like the time stopped. He covered his face with paws like he was expected explosion. However- it was quiet.
Nothing had happened. He looked in the screen and saw Blue planet that was beautiful.

However- silence. Nothing happened. He looked in disbelief at the screen and saw The Blue Planet, really wonderful. In the bottom he saw the information: "Goal- PLANET EARTH, DISTANCE 209.000.132 KILOMETERS. POSSIBILITY OF COMING TO THE GOAL DEPENDS ON THE PYRAMIDIC CRYSTALS."He added two more crystals and the journey would take about two teatric years or two hundred of Earth years. Kazom figured that they have enough energy to finish their trip, he was so happy and came closer to the coffins. Next to him was laying his best friend, Dem, who he betrayed.

He was upset with that fact so he started to cuddle the coffin of his.

The song at the end sounded like a cry of Kazom and he was still cuddling the coffin. He stood up and wiped his tears with a paw so soft-ly and gently as he did it for a million of times. He came closer to other coffins and bent. Next to Dem he saw his entire family: his wife Anitsi, his son Adan and daughter Argi. It was very powerful family of emperors. Not so far from them he saw also very important people. There was a big builder and fighter, the guardian of this family Kaj. That small group gave strength to the planet Tetran. Their bravery, loyalty and closeness to people, made the biggest threat to Artav.

Because of that they ended like persecuted into the unknown. Kazom again repeated his ability to jump on the photo deck. The deck was made from two circles one on right and the other on the left side. If the memory deck was the brain of the ship then the photo deck was the longed hand for commands. She did the commands of those who was standing on it and Kazom was the one. Kazom decided what to do. "Turn on the double protection shield, leave photo shadow of the ship and the ship covered in ultra neon." This technical genius gave such orders to photo deck that made him to move without any control. He could not register on any device like it does not appear, and there they are. That moment on the planet Tetran was registered the disappearance of the ship. Olz rushed to Altrav: "Altrav. Altrav the ship disappeared. You managed to get rid of Dem!", said and continued his mad laughing.

The Excursion

Sarajevo, 2004. The moon made all the streets to look younger. Music and rumour came from every street and city center. In the summer gardens there was like in the beehive. Neci and Mari stood on the corner of Štrosmajer's street waiting for the rest of their friends. Today, they should make a deal about their trip on the excursion. "What did I tell you? We come first as we used to!? Girls must have a good reason to be late. They are hanging a little longer with the mirror!", Neci said nervously. Mary looked at him and waved with her hand. She got bored with the answers, she was all in thoughts. Since she knew about the possible destinations for their excursion she could not sleep. When she was young she was fascinated with Egypt and its beauty, that old civilization with dry, new explanations about pyramids, letter, pharaohs. However, all those stories woke up her imagination, as well as some documentaries, and provoked explanations of such a powerful culture and civilization. Not in the craziest dream they could tell the vision of disappearance of the ancient civilization. Because of that they had insomnia and jitters because of their choice of destination. He turned towards Neci when he saw the postcard while it was coming towards them. "Good afternoon Neci and Mary! Nobody came here?", he asked in astonishment when he saw the closest person to their table as he stood up and went along.

The teacher and Mary wet and sat in front of the table. "It is good we found the place, now we can easily wait for the early risers." A class leader Melika spent her four last years with this class as a pedagogue. However, she brought into her job a lot more then she had to. She was aware of the weight of time and temptations that children had in that after-war period. That left significant trace on children so she had decided to brought herself and gave all that she had to direct them in the right way.

She was overjoyed with this generation. She hoped, with right, that she will meet it like adults in ten years time, and that they will be mature and academic people. She had a smile of joy on her face. "Teacher, would you like to order some ice-cream? Just choose a combination", Neci said like a real gentleman because he was one of the males that sat next to the teacher. They soon ordered, so they came back on the conversation about the excursion.

"Well, children. Do you have your favourite?

Spain, Italy or Egypt, let me hear you? Be free to tell me, this is democratic society."

The teacher Melika looked at Neci as she was expecting him to say it first.

Neci shifted on the chair because he did not have his own choice. He felt that the only important thing was to go on a trip together. "Well, I do not care teacher. What other friends say I will agree.", he said easily. "Neci, Neci you are always in a service of friendship and you have right. Nothing is more important than strong and true friendship. And you Mary?"

For the first time Mary said uncontrollably: "Egypt is my choice teacher! That is the country of symbols, culture and mystic. If they did not choose it I will dream my own dream in some other opportunity that is for sure.", Mary said in a dreamy and exciting voice.

Melika listened Mary and if she had heard herself in the time when she was going on her geography studies. Nothing could stop her in her intentions, because when you have dreams than you can dream it. She could understand because of that. Mary was actually the best student in her generation. The girl who early lost her father in war that took away from them on millions dreams and untold stories.

„Lovely choice, Mary! Even if I decide I would also pick Egypt for you.", she confirmed to them all because she wanted to go there, too.

"So we could hope to ride on the camels and swim in the sand.", Neci said one restless comment, and smiled.

The two same-thinkers laughed and ate their ice-cream. The murmur from the garden stopped in one moment. Neci, Mary and Melika turned to the central part of the garden and they were intrigued with the sudden silence. From the cathedral one group of strange people was coming but they had very strange clothes. For our region they looked really strange, like they came from the other planet. They were having a traditional clothes from the ancient Egypt.

"They came like we have called for them, just for those who like Egypt. Neci turned to Mary that looked without breath into the nice scene- For her, the reality was like a distant picture that disappeared from her eyes and the past is there like the present. Her thoughts were overwhelmed with the alive pictures of the ancient civilization where the central part is hers like she was the queen Hatšepsut. Her imagination would last forever if she did not hear someones load voice: "Hello!" Neci was waving in front of her eyes. "We are travelling by our own scheme, or? Where did we fly now?", he teased her. Like the summer rain suddenly fell from the sky that is how the rest of the class suddenly came near their friends and teacher.

"You are finally hear, and you did not even come late.", the teacher told with her mild voice showing her watch. They all tried to speak in one voice but she could not understand anything.

"Slowly, just slowly! Please Ema, you try to explain this late coming and hullabaloo", the teacher said and stopped any other discussion. "Well, we gathered around one tourist agency on Skenderija and looked one offer for trips.", said she in confusion. "Aaaaaand?!", lifting her left eyebrow like she had on it a symbol of question mark, teacher asked for further explanation. "Well, we have decided to go to Egypt", many voices said. "Finally, why these people here are dressed like they are from Egypt!?", Ema finished while she was looking in the group of unusually dressed people. Mary started to fell in eternity in her chair. Her inner time-machine continued his trip into that antique country. She could clearly see Nile, her pupils had widen while her thoughts were touching pyramids. Unknown thoughts and pictures that she dream about were there present.

She was trembling with her whole body because of the excitement. Everything that came later for her was not important. She deeply in her soul kept her wish because she wanted to be so close to come true. Not jokes of her friends from class, teachers advice, not even the broken glass came to Mary. Tents, dessert sand, camels, unbearable heath, oasis, sunny pyramids were the pictures that bombarded her mind. From those thoughts one could make a movie that did not get a producer or actors.

„So decision was made! We will go straight to Egypt!", their class teacher concluded louder and she noticed that her lovely student was absent i spirit. Mary looked pale in the teacher and saw her questionable look, so she smiled like she wanted to say: "Hey, here I am." The teacher continued with information.

"So we all have chosen Egypt and now the only thing that stayed is the formality about the number of passengers, and confirmation about the date of leaving. And not to forget if you give up please immediately let me know because of the ticket confirmation. ", she stood up from the chair, waved to her class and added: "Do not bother to follow me, enjoy together while you still can. In the future, you will be brought away with your new ideas, wishes, and you will go in some other school and new environments. Goodbye and be good!" Students followed their teacher with eyes and when she disappeared into the next street the hullabaloo started to happen. Like they saw "must have" , "The old Egyptians came closer to them, and offered souvenirs, jewelry and illustrated manuals about the greatest sights of Egypt. Girls looked curiously in the silver bracelets, necklaces from shiny stones and figures of alabaster. Boys were too much occupied with the story so nothing could draw their attention.

The oldest in the group of Egypt, was bent and thin, wrapped in the white cloth. He touched slowly Mary's hand and she paid attention more at him. She looked at him and she stoned when she saw the face of that stranger. "That face" she thought " well is this possible?!" In disbelief she again looked to the old mans eyes and she stayed frozen. Those eyes, nose, mouth and mild smile were the same like those to her father that was dead, Hajrudin. This man was older.

She wanted to say something and the man slowly put his forefinger on the mouth and told her to be quiet. He gave her slowly the necklace made from blue alabaster. And he said slowly: "You will understand, those who love they understand each other. Take this necklace and keep it well because you will need it. When he said that he got lost in the crowd. Mary wanted to say something but she could not leave a voice out of her mouth. She was occupied by thoughts that stood in row like dear memories and confirmed that our dearest people can never leave from us, no matter if they are not their physically. Neci again returned her to reality:

"Mary, are you going home or leaving?", he asked her mildly when he realized what was she experiencing. The only one from that class knew thoughts and plans of his dearest friend. Mary just mumbled something and she stood and walked like in the trans. She did not care because of the heath on the road, city hullabaloo or the smell of the summer. Not even the nice cognition that they will go to Egypt. Nothing from it. The face of that old man and his nice, mild words had occupied her and she was searching for a significance of all of that, but it was no worth. She could not think why would he gave her that. She just wanted to come home as soon as possible, to lay down and to calm. In one moment she thought that she should tell everything to her mom but she was indecisive. She was not convinced that it was the best solution. "No, no mom had enough of her problems. She does not need this strange story. ", she kept mumbling for herself. "What, I did not hear you well?", Neci said almost angrily because he could not understand words. His friend looked at him and smiled: "Sorry, I said more to myself, nothing important that you need to know.", she stopped his further questions.

With her hurry walk, like on the tact of military march they walked through the town, they passed near the hotel Europe, and went on the crossroad to come to the Coast. They looked down the street and because there was not so much traffic they passed towards the Latin bridge. Neci suddenly stopped and Mary looked at him asking what was going on. "Can you go home alone? I want to walk for a little while in the town.", he said sadly. Mary liked this plan because she knew that he would ask millions of questions towards the home and she did not want to talk more.

"Well, no. It is not a problem you can continue and I will go to the shop first.", she barely said her answer because she wanted to stay alone. Neci waved to her and went towards Baščaršija. "Finally alone.", Mary thought walking with tiny but fast steps towards Bistrik. In a short while she came closer to Terzibaša street and directed to the city crossroad. She saw a few neighbors and greeted them as she was well raised girl. That everyday walk by the hill imposed one the same question: "Oh, sweet Lord who said that we should live in the hill!?" That question was asked on the half of the road and whenever one of the walkers was exhausted and tired. Mary was also tired o it was good that she went to the shop first. She sighed a little while she was standing in a row and waiting for bread and milk and she asked always the same question: "Is it fresh?" She continued towards the home, but she could not stop thinking about that old man. Mom was on the yard and she was doing something around the flowers. As soon as she saw her, she left her job and asked millions of questions: "When are you travelling? Do your all friends go? In which country?, By bus or by plane? " she was so happy that her daughter will go into one foreign country and meet other cultures and people. "Easy mom! I did not come in and you ask a thousand of questions.", she hugged her and said with a smile. Mom took off her gloves, left it near the flowers and hugged Mary: "You are right, You know me I want to find everything mmediately! We must go inside the house, and you can tell me there everything. " With this sentence Mary had lost a time frame and she could not avoid answers.

A story and a dream

When she came inside the house Mary started to answer and she did not wait for her mother to ask questions again. "Like this, the whole class chose Egypt, and only if someone give up than he should tell to the class teacher", Mary said in one breath. Her mom hugged her strongly and she was overjoyed that her wish will come true. "I knew it, your dream will come true. Everything that you wish hard can come true." Mary somehow released from her mothers hug. In the few last months she refused kindness because she felt the necessity of realizing that she grew up. She looked at her mother, that sweet creature and she was aware of her efforts in all these years of her growing up. For the first time in her life she saw wrinkles on her lovely face, wrinkles left traces around her eyes and mouth. She thought that life is not fair, because it plays with destinies of some people. While combing his web, life wrote dramas, tragedies, and sometimes even comedies, leaving to people the main roles, and he did not let them to see the script for their own life. We suppose that this must be like that, because if we all know what will we act than the real mess would happen. The majority would search for an exchange because of the bad role and in the division of those roles not all people can be the main actors. Only in your own life you can be the main actor and have the main role so act the best as you could. Mary finished with her deep minds and thoughts and sat on the bed and put her head on her mothers lap. She enjoyed in the best thoughts. She lost her past revulsion towards tenderness.

Mother realized her daughters message and she started to stroke her hair, combing through the threads and cuddling it like by the comb. She knew well what was the weakness of her Mary. She knew that this ritual relaxes her favorite girl. During the war and while there was a bombarding , these cuddles and strokes, as well as fairy tales gave Mary the shelter from the biggest evil that was made by men. Mary looked at her mother as if she was expecting that something will happen during these situations. When her mother did not say anything, Mary asked: "Do these situations order story telling?"

"But stories that you did not tell me before.", she finished and did not give her mother a chance to say something. "You want some new story? There is one that I have never told you before.", mother said loud as if she was already fell into the depths of stories.

In the most beautiful town in the world, four brothers lived. The first and the oldest was doing some technical inventions. He was really wise, but introverted, and he did not like to talk much. The second by birth was an artist, he loved animals and talked with them. The third brother had a lot of money, and he never had given anything to anyone. He only took from people. He was a really a miser. The fourth brother was a cook, the good man that always gave to anyone although no one asked for it. He took from his poverty and gave to the other who probably have more money than he did. All four of them lived in one house that was left from their parents who also said that they should live in unity and concord, and to water the love like the plant in its growth and to respect one another.

Everything was as their parents left but then one day a strong wind blew and blew the house away. "What shall we do now without the house?" the oldest brother asked although he liked more the silence than the spoken word. The second one- artist answered: "You, because of your technical inventions should make necessary tools for construction, and I will draw even nicer house than we had before.

I will invite the animals to help us. The third brother- the miser only thought about his money and how to save it. And the fourth- the good man- the cook said that he will gladly help in one good deed so he claimed: "When people build house than everything is hungry. I will take care of the food for us and animals." The next day, they started to build it. The oldest one as it was planned, made tools that were necessary for construction. The second one started to draw the house plan and he called for his animal friends. The third hid behind the tree to count his money, and then he came to those three brothers and gave them three worthless pennies. The fourth came to the fire and wanted to cook some lunch. The first one said: I need more money, I must buy the material for tools that was missing." The three of them looked in astonishment because the older had never spoken so much. The second one said: "I need paper and even pencils. So I need money for it."

The third only had an evil smile because he did not even consider to give them his own money. The fourth one saw that they will not get any money of their brother, sat on one old stump and started to cry silently: "We do not have money for food to cook, we will not have anything to eat, not we or animals. We will die from starvation."

The third brother was still smiling counting his money. The older brother turned to the third and said: "Our father and mother taught us how to divide everything."

The second added: "They taught us how to love and take good care for others. They left this as an inheritance."

The fourth stopped his crying and said: "They told us to love and respect each other."

The third did not do anything. Then the night fell, and they went to sleep under the sky full of stars. Very soon they fell asleep and started to dream their own dreams. The first one had a dream that he found everything necessary for his tools. The second one that he has plenty of papers and pencils for his construction sketch. The third one counted his money in his dream and wiped it with a handkerchief in order to keep it shiny. But suddenly coins disappeared and he started to cry. The fourth one was so happy in his dream because he cooked food for thousand of hungry children. While he was cooking he was also telling them the greatest stories. Animals fell asleep and dreamed something. One thought that it was in the forest, the other that it was in the air, the third that it was in the water and the fourth one on the meadow. When the morning came they could not believe their own eyes. In front of them there was a house. The most beautiful house that no one had see before, and around the house a wonderful garden. You can not imagine how many different flowers was planted there. The four brothers were standing in front of that wonderful view like someone hit them. They could not imagine something like that, nice house, barn and garden. They all stood like frozen and nodded their heads in order to see better from all sides. Then the third one said: "Look! This house only has three floors and our house had

four floors!" They all looked at him like he was not from this planet and again they turned to the house: ""Really, the house has only three floors!", the second one confirmed.

The fourth one said: "Come on inside the house to see it well." When they came to the main door they saw the inscription:

I FLOOR- THE OLDEST BROTHER
II FLOOR- THE SECOND BROTHER
III FLOOR- THE FOURTH BROTHER

They all looked to each other because they did not understand who was playing with them all. And the third brother cried all aloud: "Oh, poor me, poor me! I do not have a place in this house, where will I go now?!" All three of them started to comfort him and convinced him that the house is big enough for all of them. Then they heard one unknown voice out of no where:

"Love, kindness and faith always get awards!" The voice stopped and then continued: "Stinginess, envy and malice always get its punishment!" Brother looked in disbelief. The voice again said: "The third brother will go on the desert island to count the waves that hit into the coast, to try to handle his pennies and coins and to realize the material uselessness. To learn that only friendship, honesty, love and truth are eternal and stable."

The first one turned to the second one, the second one to the fourth one and they saw that the third brother disappeared. And so these three brothers lived in a unity like all brother should live." Mom finished her story and she saw that her daughter fell asleep. She grabbed the pillow and put it under Mary and she just turned and continued her sleep. Dream quickly caught the man and he could easily dream something fast.

They say that dream does not last enough as a blink of an eye but so many pictures and events are put inside that only talk about it lasts forever if you remember your dream. And those people who remember their dreams are rare. Mary just dreamed about her old dream. She saw again that old man, old ships on Nile and one creature not a man or a beast.

She heard a loud song of slaves who were hungry and thirsty and were forced to do difficult jobs because of the pharaoh and his military whips. They all dreamed one same dream, they wanted to get their home again. Indeed, there are many different dreams but only in the service of those who sleep, in order to fulfill their wishes. However, only in our dreams we have a balance between reality and those that we wish for in human life. If the dream does not exist, many people, if not all of them, would be ruined by their consciousness. So this dream that Mary had, was a product of wish, love, fear and impatience.

A strange passanger

The next morning she was relaxed and ready for her trip preparations. Soon she heard from her teacher about the trip and its journey. "I hope you make all preparations for the trip, we are going tomorrow at ten. We should meet at the airport at eight. Turn on your alarm at least two hours before in order to get there on time. See you tomorrow. Goodbye."

Mary said something like goodbye and continued to check prepared things. She told to herself aloud: "Do not forget the necklace from alabaster! You can forget anything else but not that!" She pulled out the necklace and put it on her neck. A wallet with her money and photos of her dear people soon find its place in the jacket with many pockets that were ready for putting only necessary things. Mom slowly told her some advice's and counted things that one could not leave on such a big trip without. "Mom please, you should not worry. I know what is the most important. I have a list here, when I pack I then cross the thing from the list. ", she looked at here worriedly and she wanted her not to worry so much.

"Okay then I will go, because I do not want to disturb my world passenger.", mom said with a smile and found herself one other interesting thing to do. Very soon, darkness fell on the sky and in the houses like by the command lights were turned on. Mary wanted to leave the impression that she was a calm person who was not giving any attention to the future trip and her mothers worry. She finished her dinner quickly, drank some juice and went into her room. "Mom, I will go earlier to bed because we should be on the airport at eight o clock in the morning. Good night."

Her mother spent a few minutes more over tapestry, put it on the sofa, took a clock from the drawer and winded the clock. "I will order telephone alarm because it could not harm." she commented for herself. She turned lights off in the house. When the man is in expectation of something it seemed that the time stopped although it passed by normally. Mary did not feel that way. As soon as she laid down she fell asleep. Morning waking up, rushing into the toilet, brushing and putting on her clothes, mother and her small advice's only told Mary that she got a trip in front of her. When she checked everything, she took her luggage, said goodbye to her mother, kissed her and waved from the end of the street where she was waiting fora taxi. The day was wonderful. The sun heated the air so strong and on the sky she saw clouds in different shape. These were like some lambs in the field. Mary waited for the taxi and entered in it, then she gave the instructions to the driver and said where to drive to. The engine of this car gave a good speed of and entered the narrow streets of Sarajevo. She came on the proper destination. When they came, Mary saw many familiar faces. She thought how good it was that she did not come the last. Her teacher came closer because she knew how excited she was and calmed her down: "Mary, be patient, a few of them is late."

From the closest group she heard a music from a radio. Young people did not care about the length of the road and possible danger, or problems that could happen. Youth is the most beautiful part of the life. Carelessness, joy, and friendship were their biggest worries. When the teacher announced that they all came, she asked her students to board the bus. They loaded all the luggage in and went towards the airport. During this short ride, their teacher gave them a few notifications about the weather, temperature, time zone, as well as the duration of the flight. Some students asked many questions like: "If we are flying over the Mediterranean sea, what will happen if the engine breaks? Do we have enough boats for the continuation of a trip?" Those jokes and questions came on the laugh. Their teacher found it useful because she knew that every fear can be defeated if they consider it through jokes. Then they heard a voice of a driver: "Young world passengers we came on wanted destination. Please go out of the bus. Try not to leave your things here and I wish you a nice trip! And just to know I will be waiting for you when you return and I hope that you will bring me at least a bottle of sand from a desert.", he laughed in the end and waved to them. The whole bunch of voices greeted him and promised a gift. "Come on. Do not be slow and take a bigger trolley. More things can be put in it. Hurry up we must pass the passport control.", the teacher told her students.

Journey, journey, journey, that was the only thing in the heads of passengers, and advice's of their teacher nobody listened. The real rush came when they passed with trolleys to the central part of building. Soon they heard the notice from loudspeaker: "We ask from passengers on the line Sarajevo- Cairo to approach passport control. Departure is scheduled for 11:30. We beg passengers..."

The teacher mimed and pushed some students to hurry through the passport control, as well as the last check of students before they came in the plane.

At the end they beginning boarding the plane. Students were very patient and did not push or tease each other. They stopped joking. They entered in the strange silence and trying to find their seats- with the number on their tickets without words. Except of the students that were going on excursion , in the plane many other passengers were travelling to the same destination. They mutually comment- ed the comfort in the plane and reasons why they have chosen this journey.

Like they did not have a fear at all, and if they are sitting in the tram, but this could not be told for the students because they have never used a plane before. Soon, all the passengers sat on their seats and flight attendants started their procedure by explaining it all and what to do in some extreme situations. When they finished, picture symbols were turned on and it told the passengers that they must use their safe belt. A captain announced the duration of the flight and the countries that they will fly over. He welcomed them. All passengers did what was necessary for the safe flight and felt the engine that was turned on. The bravest of them decided to look through the window while the runaway was escaping in front of their eyes. The plane climbed faster and fast- er until it came on the right speed and lifted first its upper and then lower part. This huge machine came on the proper height and took its direction.

The whole that situation was followed by one passenger that was sitting in his own seat. Who is that unknown passenger? He was wrapped into a black silk scarf that hid his face and one could only see his dark glasses, and pursed lips. He had on his head a black and white hat that can be drawn to time when in this world only charlton dance was popular. This packed up guy only looked on someone who is full of secrets. After the flight started, the atmo- sphere in the plane was more relaxed. One could hear even a few jokes. They forgot their own fears and even those who were on their first flight, quickly got used to the plane and flying. After half an hour they already seemed like pas- sengers that fly for hundreds of times. Mary stirred in her seat and turned her head to the seat where the strange passenger was sitting. She felt that he was observing her thoroughly

although she could not say it exactly because of his glasses.

Mary quickly looked somewhere else.

She did not feel comfortable. Questions multiplied in her head: "Who is he? What does he do? Is he a Bosnian or Arabian? Why did she feel so strange around him? Is her destiny connected with his?" She felt like he is familiar to her.

She looked at him again and she saw an empty seat. She started to look around the plane in a confusion. When she did not manage to find this strange passenger she turned to the window. Someone touched her shoulder. She turned unwillingly because she thought it was one of her friends from the class. She was astonished. The stranger was sitting next to her and showed her to be quiet with his finger. He opened the palm of his other hand and she saw figures of pyramids.

"Do you want to find out how did they make them? You are silent, does this mean that you are afraid? You do not have a reason for that. The stranger looked at her and offered her the truth about the most mysterious thing in the world. Mary was thinking what to do. At the end those were just miniatures of pyramids. Toys. "What can he explain about it?", Mary wondered. The stranger was still holding an open hand but with one difference. Around pyramids one could see a sand and camels. Unbelievable but obviously that this stranger had some strange powers. Mary tried to find with her

look- the teacher and what she saw made her tremble.

All the passengers were in some kind of trans, they were like frozen, immovable with a glassy gaze. "Only you can see and hear this", the stranger said again.

"You are chosen from millions to know the truth. Decide quickly so we can go to the journey", the stranger said leaving Mary no choice. The voice was familiar but she did not know from where. Why this happened to her? What to do?

"Then we will go to the biggest adventure in the history?", the stranger said again and smiled. The decision was taken with such an easiness and this made one invisible bag on the plane that was just about to explode. "We will go." Mary gave her hand to a stranger and felt some unbearable heath on her palm. The stranger moved his left hand from his body towards the pilot cabin.

As he did it, the right side of the plane opened and they saw soft clouds as a faithful followers of dreams. Movement of his right hand, like he wanted to make waves, formed wonderful stairs and led to the place where the stranger wanted.

et me take you", the stranger said offering his hand. here was no return. However she was decisive in situations and she proved it. Mary took his hand and almly: "Come on! Of course, now is the real time for y adventure!" then the stranger came together with down the stairs and sang:

When you come on this world and look
You do not know what you gave or took
And the picture in galaxy goes
All that are up see your actions close
You have a head so think well
Why many of them from sadness fell
And let your hands to fly
Like the bees on the flowers and sky
Meadow full of flowers
Let choose one as ours
Pull up your gray sleeves
Color your life like flowers and leaves
Nothing can escape from you
From books you should learn, too
And when everything to this world you give
To the galaxy come and with those pictures live
For grief will be surely late
Wandering in galaxy will be your fate.

The stranger finished the song and asked Mary curiously: "What do you think about the song?" While he was expecting her answer they were still descending or better to say slipping down the stairs. Mary listened well the song and had expectation. "The song is good, full of messages and wisdom, but also sorrows, but this song was written for someone special. Am I right?"

"Ha, ha, ha...You are really wise when you ask those things." the stranger said happily. "You see, there where we are going maybe you will hear this song and maybe not", he said mysteriously. Mary did not pay attention at first on some details. She was not sure what did she saw properly in that moment. Because of the song she did not pay attention that their clothes is changing and transforming through different ages. "Can you explain this?" Mary asked her passenger showing on the clothes that was changed every time when they stepped down the stairs. That moment Mary had wonderful dress from the age of baroque and the stranger was also clothed in the clothes from that age.

"You see, my telling about your wisdom and smartness were
not for nothing. Many people would not notice what happened because of the excitement that follows every adventure, but you do
not miss anything.", he said with pleasure.
"I can tell you that we are travelling in the past because of your love
towards pyramids and Egypt, so every stair represents significant period of that country and history. We stood here in the 17th century so
take a close look what life could we live there in that time." He said that
and clapped his hands. Suddenly they came in the palace that looked
like it was a part of some wonderful fairy tale and that there lived
prince and princess. Music gave the additional impression, while they
were slipping over the floor and enjoying in the magnificent comfort.
" Ooooh, well that is really wonderful. What kind of costumes, what
elegance!", she said thrilled.

The stranger just smiled and lifted his hand to stop the time and suddenly music and dancing couples stopped. The whole hall looked
like a photo. "Here, now you can come closer and take a look at costumes, their color, material. You are in time machine and it stopped
in the era of baroque."That is the period that was the best in art."
he explained the short period of time where they fell into. "I would
like to go to an old Egypt, and about this period I would rather
talk in return.", Mary said impatiently. "I am not surprised with
your wish to see an old Egypt but I thought that we should
make a small break, a pause to smell also the other eras. But
as you wish. Your wishes are my command." the stranger
mildly bent towards Mary and again clapped with his
hands but this time twice. Like with the speed of stars
they both again went on the journey. Because of the
speed they could not realized anything except of
the colors of these time periods.

In the next moment the journey stopped. Daily light was exchanged with colors of rainbow. Mary trembled like the leaf on the wind- what she saw did not leave any other option except that they came where they needed. "Finally Egypt", opening her hands Mary went straight to the first right street. It was a canal where the water was flowing. In front of Mary and the stranger the big valley was opened and it went all along the blue water. It was not just any kind of water- it was Nile itself, river among rivers, the life for many Egyptians that lived all over this fertile plain. Mary hurried to come near the canal. Then she heard some unknown voices. "Slowly, do not hurry! I must give you few advice's!", the stranger said rushing behind Mary. Mary did not hear his words. Her legs were already in the field of wheat, golden ear of corns like the sun in the moon. Voices of somebody brought her there. Guessing that those voices were very close, Mary turned down the ears of cor and saw a girl and a boy that were probably as old as she was. In that moment they stopped talking like they were scared of her. "Oh, oh", panting and flushed the stranger came. When he saw her accompanied by this couple he said: You are so stubborn! You do not want to hear advice but you came here unprepared and scared residents of old Egypt.", he scolded her. " What to say to them? Will they understand me?", she asked stranger while those two young people

looked at them with a great interest. They have lost their previous fear. "I wanted to tell you that but I could not stop you!?", the stranger said angrily, so he put his hand between those two people and Mary and said: "There now you can speak with them. No problem." This young couple understood the gesture and started to talk.

"Your hair is like the color of the sun"- the boy said.
"And the color of your skin is like the color of milk"- the girl said.
"You are tall and young as we are"- the boy continued.
"You have a long step"- the girl said.
"From which kingdom do you come from?"- the boy asked.
"Do you have a brother by blood?"- the girl asked.
" Is he coming with a shiny ship?"- the boy asked again.
"Is he faster than a blink of an eye?"- the girl asked.
Then again started like in one voice:
"Do you have pyramids that can be seen from distance?"
"In the castle do you have doors, are all golden?"
"Do you look in the sky if the ships are coming?"
"You know for sure the way to your home
To meet your planet..."

They stopped suddenly in the same way as they began. Mary looked in disbelief how the tears fell from their faces, and as soon as their tears fell on the ground it transformed in crystals. It jingled like gold coins when they are spilled all over the stone path. Mary bent and took crystals and then she offered it to the couple: "Take this, it is yours! I have never seen something like this before. Is there a secret of this or some kind of magic?", Mary asked them.

The boy laughed and his teeth were as white as pearls.

"We do not want to explain but you can just made a fist with our crystals in it and wish to know everything about us. In one moment you will get all information about us."

She made a fist in a wish to know everything about them. Destiny wanted to put in Mary's memory all about royal family and their unscrupulous exile. When she opened her eyes she offered them hands friendly. She knew everything about them in that moment.

Architectural wonder

„I know you, You are Adan." said Mary pointing at the boy. "And you are Argi." she looked at the girl. "I know everything about you! From which planet do you come from and your names, parents and what brought you here. It is my pleasure to know you, we will be a good friends." Mary said in one breath like the wind. Adin and Argi came closer and put their palms on her head.

One unusual flow of information started to go into her head again, this time from Mary's time and future as well as some technological inventions that were not invented in that moment.

"Woow this is fantastic!!! Is it possible that those inventions are right in front of us and that we do not see it!?", Mary said in astonishment. Adan and Argi took Mary cheerfully for her hands and took her in the direction of the big building that was the biggest in the environment. Mary was all excited and rushed up, she suspected what was that about and he heart started to beat faster, on her face one could see first drops of sweat. She was more and more nervous with every other step. They went out from the golden corns on the path that was made from the ground that was polished to perfection.

The view took out the breath. The central part of the building looked so enormous and gave the impression of even taller building. That maybe would not be nothing special if it is not about the world miracle. The pyramid. Mary from excitement could not say a word. She turned to Argi and Adan and gesticulated in a wish to show her excitement. Then she said something: "Wow, fantastic, unbelievable! I would give everything if this planet can see these buildings!", she said for herself. "Adan, Argi", she called for them. "Tell us Mary why are you so upset?", Adan asked. Mary looked in astonishment. "How can you ask me that?", Mary asked fast. "The building of pyramids is a miracle by itself, the miracle is big and the technique looks so bad?", she said. Adan looked at her in astonishment. "How can you say that the technique is bad? How can you conclude that and you did not even see us while we were building it!?", the young man said angrily. "What else can I know!?

We know everything about pyramids and its building", Mary said because she thought on all those things that they have learned in school, although she was never satisfied with those explanations. They were coming closer to pyramids, and they were not tired at all. They heard different voices from the construction site and it looked like the biggest composition. Mary than figured out that they were close the construction site and looked in a wonderful pictures in front of her. "Really magical atmosphere that it can not be more magical! Like in the cinema when we see a spectacle of history. Those wonderful colors that were spilled in front of her eyes were something most wonderful that one could see. From her strong wish she peeked into every corner, looked at every color and heard every sound. Like she floated through the air and did not touch the ground. Every thought that she wanted to see something was like the command for the walk in that direction. Mary quickly found out how that worked and started to behave like that. Then she saw the real truth about building and pyramids. All previous theories and science explanations fell under those construction site.

Theories about slaves like they were forced to work, and the technique that was based on the physical effort and a few ropes and boards looked ridiculous on those sites. This was something like the advanced construction site that could be measured as the contemporary technique used in nowadays civilization. With the right counting one could measure even that those people from Egypt were far away in technology and buildings from our twenty-first century.

Mary just could not understand: "How those inventions could not pass on the next generations?"

Of course, she knew that she was not on this place for nothing, because this was the right place for answers. Adan and Argi waved to her from the ground and gave her sign to step down on the Earth. Mary understood at the end their intention and stepped down: "This overcomes my greatest imagination! It can not be compared to anything! Great, magnificent!", from the great excitement her voice trembled and in her eyes one could only see pyramids.

No construction site, not even this one, lacked the number of employees, and the hustle and bustle made the construction environment pulsating and alive. On this construction site, however, there was a slight difference. The workers here were dressed in strange work suits. Over the upper part of the body to below the knee, they had tunics of pure silk with certain applications that determined the status and expertise of the worker.

But the strangest of all was the head protection. Now it was clear to Mary why there was a wrong explanation of science and researchers about the image of these workers.

Masks resembling dog heads covered the workers' heads. Modern science has explained how it was the priests who wore such robes during the mummification ceremony, i.e. the death of the ruler. There was no need to ask for an explanation, it was just

It seems simple that it couldn't be simpler, but the question arises, what is the use of breathing masks for workers when there is enough oxygen on Earth?

The explanation for that too is too simple and defeats the complicated science that, in the absence of quality answers, offers solutions that correspond to its weak vision.

Of course, no normal person will claim that stone slabs weighing twenty tons or more are lifted by a few workers.

Something else was happening here. The workers with masks were actually working in an airless environment! Yes, believe it or not, in airless space!

"This is how it goes," Mary said aloud. "So, in an area that is 1000 meters in diameter on four sides and 400 meters high, everything takes place under a glass box. Air is pumped under the glass box so that the huge boulders appear as light as a piece of paper. The workers have a key role in directing the boulders to the places that were marked with green laser lights."

According to what Mary told us, it turns out that building pyramids is no more difficult than building a house.

Mary could not bear to comment on this strange work that she had seen with her own eyes: "So that's the point! It is clear to me why in the drawings found in the tombs they wear masks over their faces! Well, they're kind of oxygen tanks!"

she said, turning to Adan and Arga.

"You're right about the dog masks, they really are air tanks, but you mention some tombs with pictures of these workers?!", Adan looked questioningly at Mary«.

In a moment, Mary realized that she had returned to the time of the ancient Egyptians, and not the other way around, so the subsequent knowledge about the pyramids as well as the drawings could not possibly have been known by these two. The gap of centuries between them created mental blocks.

She realized that she should switch to a completely different topic: "Will you introduce me to your parents, I would be so glad?", she asked hastily and somewhat awkwardly.

Such a quick switch from one topic to another could not go unnoticed. Argy said: "Mary, I hope you could see at least a fraction of our civilization, which we in no way wanted to show otherwise, even though your brain sent a request for just such distorted images." Girl stopped only for a brief second as if she wanted Mary to think about what she said then continued: "We have the ability to transcribe your thoughts into words. However, we did not do so out of a deep conviction of your sincerity. I hope we haven't made a mistake, am I right?" Argy finished with a childish little hint of anger. Regardless of culture, language, skin color, girls like Argi have established themselves as the original characters of girls from fairy tales. That's how she left a strong impression on Meri, who was upset when she heard Arga's explanation. She tried to think of something else so as not to give away the period she came from. However, she did not succeed, because Adan continued the questioning game.

"You heard what Argy said, and I'll just add that we know you come from the distant future and somehow know our story, its beginning and end." However, that view doesn't have to be correct, that's why you're here. We offer you honesty, but we also expect the same from you," Adan finished the sentence perfectly calmly. This truly exceeded all of Mary's expectations. It was quite clear to her that she had to tell the complete truth to every question that would be put to her in this space and time. Suddenly, something occurred to her: she remembered the interesting stranger with whom she had started this strange journey. Se began to turn in all directions, looking for a stranger, but she did not see him.

"You must be looking for a Time Keeper, ha, ha, ha...", Adan and Arghi laughed sweetly. "Don't be afraid, he's here somewhere." When you want to come back, he will be with you," added Argy.

"Well, I'm just checking where he is," Mary

said quickly, trying to hide her discomfort. The moment she realized that she had arrived at the place of her desires and imagination, the discomfort disappeared and a single "Woooow!" escaped from her throat. "Tell me I'm dreaming, tell me!", she uttered in one breath, turning around, raising and lowering her hands, all of this resembled the dance of some forgotten ancient civilization.

Can something be older, ie. more ancient than ancient Egypt!? What fascinated Mary so much? We will stay here a little longer to be able to count all the miracles that Mary saw. The very configuration of the terrain dictated the overall view at the very entrance to the valley, which, as we said, was flooded with wheat fields. Between the fields and the river, there was a narrow path, barely visible to the human eye, that led up a small hill towards the pyramids. Coming out on a huge plateau, two smaller pyramids that could not be seen from the valley would suddenly emerge in front of the traveler.

They had sharp edges from the ground to the top, covered with black marble polished to perfection, and just one look at these geometric mountains created an imaginary scene in front of the visitor, as if at that moment they would start their internal engines and take off. They were just waiting for the command. Such an image was enhanced by the hot condensed air that flickered around the pyramids.

Behind the pyramids, the valley opened in all its greenery, blue water and wonderful buildings.

A city lay below. It was a megalopolis that could not be measured with the eyes, it was lost where the sky and the earth touch.

For Mary, it should not be surprising to see a city of this size, because even in our time there are dozens of multi million-people cities. But this city had a magical effect. It was pure architectural perfection.

The buildings were constructed in an unusual way. Unprecedented shapes and strange styles. They were mostly ring-shaped buildings that leaned on each other and stood even though there was no solid support. So, dozens of rings were multiplied by connecting to each other without real contact or any connections from building materials. They seemed to be floating Arches in the shape and color of the rainbow passed above them, except that these buildings had their beginning and end in the ground.

The very entrance to the city was made up of buildings like elephant tusks. They were placed in two rows - one opposite the other. All the buildings were soft colors with lots of glass surfaces, and the colors varied from grass green, pale blue

like the deep sea, soft pink to blinding white that gave the impression as if there was no glass at all. Going towards the center of the city, one could see numerous large and unusual trees of large trunks, very tall with a huge canopy of turquoise leaves.

At their base were seedlings of all kinds of flowers that had the strange ability to transform into any flower of any color. It was enough for a passer-by to think of a shape or a certain color, and in the same instant the plants would change into what the lucky person wanted.

Mary commented more to herself: "Now I understand how the traffic light came into being!" Watching these miracles, a man put himself in an incomprehensible situation of not believing his own eyes. The center itself presented an unforgettable image: an obelisk all three hundred meters high was planted in a large fountain that spewed out water in six-pronged jets to the rhythm of wonderful music. Depending on the tempo and speed of the music, the water rose to the top of the obelisk, only to descend halfway the next moment, thus changing the height of the jet. It would not be so unusual if the water itself could not control every drop in its stream. Mary rubbed her eyes in disbelief at what she saw.

One of the many passers-by who liked the music approached the fountain and bowed, extending his right hand towards the water. A gesture like when a lady is invited to dance. Indeed, this was also an invitation to dance. The water from the waterfall formed into a dancer's partner, and she and a passer-by danced to the music, sliding on the marble pavement. This dancing couple attracted the attention of other passers-by, so they also chose partners and danced.

It was a breathtaking sight for anyone with a sense of the beautiful and elegant. Music and dancing in the open air, a life of a lighter rhythm, indulging the senses of life. Mary unconsciously clapped her hands, giving support and tact to the dancers. It was indeed a memorable experience for her. The melody will soon become quieter and fade away. When the music stopped, the dancers thanked their partners, and the one who invited the water jumper to the dance politely moved away and bowed, kissed the water's hand and, look at that, the dancer remained completely dry! What else can I say but a real miracle!

Adan lightly touched Mary's shoulder, she flinched: "Don't be afraid, you got too carried away. How do you like our city?"»

O She looked at him in astonishment and thought: "This guy must be joking!" Something like this would knock even the coldest man out of his shoes."

"It's nothing," Argy interjected. In order to divert Mary's attention to herself, she swiped her hand at shoulder height twice through the air like a wiper. Suddenly, a screen appears out of nowhere.

"There are various possibilities to get information here. You saw the way the colors and shape of the flowers change. In the same way, you can get information - pictorial, spoken

and written, and all accompanied by the music you like,' the all-important little girl hastily blurts out, as only little girls can, while remaining sweet.

For the umpteenth time, Mary was delighted by new evidence of the development of this rich civilization. She moved to the side, and began to hop on one leg. Not wasting another moment, Argy started jumping like Mary. Hop, hop, hop, and every next one after her.

Adan watched this, for him, somewhat silly sight in surprise. As this senselessness continued, unable to look at her any longer, he said: "Let's go on, leave these stupid games, please!", he somehow managed to say it, when he saw dozens of children hopping on one leg following Mary and Argy.„

"Mary, please stop jumping! I don't know why you even started," Adan pleaded.«

Mary had just turned a circle and was hopping straight towards Adan. Breathing pretty much heavily, she began to answer him: "You see, despite my best will to understand that all that I saw is mere reality, I check again that I am not dreaming, and this hopping on one leg comes to me as the best check", when she finished with the answer, she found herself right in front of Adan.

She looked him straight in the eyes. She slid her gaze down his pupils and it seemed to her as if he was falling through some deep well. Then he began to experience the virtual world. In fact, Mary absorbed all the images that Adan's brain had registered since he was born. All Adan's experiences were reflected on Mary's face. If the events were sad and Mary's face was sad, if the event was happy, Mary's face was smiling. Suddenly, as it had begun, the projection stopped and the two young people found themselves back in the reality of their time.

"This with the screen really works, I can get any information!" It's enough just to think about what I want," sh excitedly addressed the girl Arga. All startled because Mary addressed her for one of many achievements, Argy hastened to answer: "Here, this is how you can go into the future, go back to the past, find out what kind of life you will live, how science will develop, simply, to everything that you are interested in, you'll be able to get an answer", the little girl finished with a smile. Arga's words made Mary think about what it would be good to know, without knowing it yet. Soon, her brain is flooded with wishes that would have been impossible to realize in her time, she would not even be allowed to say them, because she would be considered crazy. Just as she was about to think of her wish, she heard a murmur, turned and saw a huge number of people standing in a perfect row. Somewhere right in the middle of that mass was a golden carriage pulled by white horses. There were exactly twelve of them - six in a pair. They were also decorated, and their main equipment was also made of gold. Another picture appeared in front of Mary, as if from the most beautiful dreams.

Adan warned her: "That's our father Dem and mother Anitsi coming to greet you." They were informed that you came from another time and space", he pointed with his hand at the column that was getting closer and closer. Mary gasped in surprise. The royal family is coming for her. Hastily she said, "Are there any customs I should know, please tell me Argy?"

"You don't have to be afraid of making a fool of yourself. Look at me, and whatever I do, you do too," Argi chirped cheerfully.

The column was indeed closing in on them. Mary could already make out the faces of the people in the carriage. The column stopped. They spread themselves left and right, making the letter V, so that the carriage with Arga and Adan's parents came into the foreground.

Dem stood up and held out his hands to these three children

This day
For you dream, hooray
You do not have anything to say
Open your heart to happiness
Centuries are between and away
In the God salvation came
We should believe in everything like fame
They did not know truth, imagination was made
Slaves did jobs and were not paid
That does not exist in this town
Our pictures and signs were down
They said I am a pharaoh

By the name Kefren narrow
And pyramids I built
In that new life to be fulfilled.
I must beg pictures to solve
Inventions in the science and resolve
And you girl Mary, come to me
Your blonde hair is great to see.
Now you know the truth real
Do not give a judgement you seal
Give them five time
Your explanations tougher than crime
Let them think what is day and night
They must go to see other world and sight
Because of that until this last
Sleep and dream something nice and fast.

As Dem finished with this sort of message in the song, Mary saw out of the corner of her eye that Argy was putting her right hand over his heart and bowing slightly. She immediately understood that it was a sign of respect, and she did the same. She did not manage to see Adan, but concluded that he did the same.

Mary slowly approached the golden carriage, stroked the first horse in the carriage, and addressed Dem:

"When I go back to my time, how can I explain the greatness and progress of this civilization without being called crazy?" What should I do to realize that this is not a dream, what?", many questions came to her and she was impatiently waiting for the answer.

Dem slowly removes the traditional headband and runs his fingers through his snow-white hair. He looked thoughtful. With a light movement of his hand, he called the guard Agans, whispered something to him and pointed in the direction of the palace that dominated the city, because, like the pyramids, it was located on a hill, just on the opposite side of the valley. Agnes turned to the accompanying retinue, clapped his hands and said something to them, and they turned in silence and headed towards the palace.

The guard signaled to Dem that he had passed on the instructions, stood next to him and became his shadow.

"Dear Mary, here, I asked my closest collaborators to allow us some solitude, because your questions require very meaningful answers, practical and with good evidence of credibility," he finished and extended his hand to Mary. Soon she plunged her hand into Dem's, feeling the warmth and softness of his hand at the same time.

"Let me become your teacher in a way in one easy walk and help you with your dilemmas." You can start with your questions," Dem suggested to her, and they slowly started walking. They passed the first few steps in silence. Mary was thinking of what question to start with, and Dem was expecting them.

"We were taught at school about the beginning and end of the life of people, plants or animals. If this is how we end, what is the meaning and purpose of the beginning, and even the end?", began Mary.

Dem took a deep breath and thought that the question of origin and disappearance is always first. In fact, everyone is happy when they appear, but it is confusing when the time of disappearance comes. His eyes got a slightly lighter shade at that moment.

"You say that the school is, um, an educational institution that allows you to expand your horizons and acquire new knowledge." Well, you see, the only drawback of that education is grading." He paused there for a while, stroking Mary's hair.

"It is difficult to rise above the emotional, visual and sensory. Teachers are human and make mistakes in everything, including so-called objective assessment." His voice, calm and quiet like a lullaby, relaxes Mary, who somehow becomes sure that she will get the right answers.

Dem continued, "What I've told you so far will make a lot of sense when I'm done with the answers," he said, plucking his gray pointy beard. Mary waited carefully for the continuation.

And as it only happens in stories, when wise men and wizards would make certain pauses in their answers in order to arouse as much attention as possible, it is reflected in this moment as well. His fingers made a single motion through the air as if to indicate that a sequel was coming.

"We will take rain as an example. So, at a certain time, it starts to rain over your city, sometimes small and boring, and sometimes heavy rain drops, which quickly stop."

"So you don't know when it will start raining or how long it will last." Only the Creator knows that! One part falls into the rivers, and the other to water the crops. Basically, it gets a place on the ground, like everything else," while saying all this, Dem gestured with his hands making movements like you do pantomime.

"Of course, now there is an explanation that you also know - after the rain, the sun shines, and there is nice evaporation from the rivers and the ground." The same drops that fell in the rain, you know the further sequence of things, don't you?" asked Mary, who stirred without expecting to participate in the answers herself. "Well, I guess the evaporation creates clouds from which it rains again," said Mary with satisfaction.

Dem laughed: "You see, the answer to everything is always close, you just have to think rationally, so this answer also has a sequel."

Another short break followed.

"We said that those newly formed clouds bring new rain with the same drops that played their role in that place, so to speak," he started making movements with his hand again as if something was walking or walking. "These or those clouds, with the help of the wind, their good friend, go over your city over some other or over some forest or similar and what happens? That one of the many drops that fell over your city begins to fall again." Dem fell into a great fire explaining the origin and disappearance. "And so, my Mary, it rains repeatedly up and down and there you have the same drops on another continent. Is this kind of answer enough for a smart woman?", Dem looked at Mary, expecting a reaction. Mary's face shone with happiness. This Dem's story simplified things for her about origin and disappearance.

"So, when we disappear, we are born somewhere

53

else. Is that your answer, Deme?"

"Ha, ha, ha," Dem laughed heartily. "Exactly. No life is created to disappear forever, it is only reborn in order to be created again in a new environment and with new friends", he says this somewhat wistfully.

Mary realized that no man, not even one with this kind of knowledge, is immune to longing, that is, to the thought of those closest to him who are no longer with him. In fact, an explanation like this gave Mary a special sense of calm. For her, it meant confirmation that her father was alive, just somewhere else, as Dem said. Such a graphic explanation could be applied to every subsequent question.

Mary wished for a moment that all people succeed in getting answers to questions they feel are unanswerable. The worst thing is to be empty and think that you are only in this world to suffer, which is not true in any case.

With interesting explanations and Dem's theatrical movements, Mary didn't even notice that they had reached the large pyramid that was already finished, which left her in shock.

"Is this possible?! You completed the pyramid in less than two hours, I can't believe it!", Mary said in astonishment. Not wanting to spoil her astonishment, Dem paused for a moment, and only then tried to answer.

"It's clear, Mary, that preparation is more than half the job, so it was important to make stone blocks for the construction of this pyramid." It had to be the perfection of cutting and processing," said Dem significantly, then continued: "There must not be the slightest mistake, because all the work falls into the water. Once that is done, the rest is basically a formality. You saw part of the construction."

"Yes, yes, yes, of course," answered Mary, who for the umpteenth time went from understanding and quieting her emotions to being surprised again.

"Our technology is at such a level that building with any natural material is not a problem for us. The problem here on planet Earth arises when you want to leave traces of the culture of achievement as a civilization" Dem said disappointedly.

"I don't understand, is someone physically preventing such a thing or is it something else?" Mary said impatiently.

Waving his hand as if to say: No, that's not the point, Dem continued: "Mary, it's about the grounds, the areas where we've tried everything to build our pyramids and the city." These are all areas that would have been destroyed by earthquakes and human hands after a few centuries", Dem choked a little here.

Mary asked him carefully if he needed anything and if he was okay. "It's fine. I'll be fine. Every time I talk about this I get a little upset. To continue, for the most part, this is the only area that will not suffer major erosions or any displacements in terms of the encroachment of another civilization that would destroy this one."

"I don't understand: terrain, displacements, another civilization, what are you trying to tell me?"

"I want to say that I know what will happen to any culture and civilization that makes great achievements, and that all this was done without bullying anyone on the basis of achievements and technique, as you yourself have had the opportunity to see, while history as a science will assert otherwise," said Dem a little angrily. Mary listened intently, realizing that Dem had a point. After all, history was written by the victors, the conquerors who destroyed other cultures and civilizations.

Dem continues his monologue: "I firmly assert that, because the many cultures that come after us will not be interested in preserving it," he turned to the city, pointing at it. "Here, look at the perfection of construction and ecology, look closely! Can you imagine that one day there won't be any at all?!", said Dem in a trembling and tearful voice.

Such human greatness and kindness, yet he cries. No wonder, if he is sure that such beauties will disappear.

"Well, how come that you, Dem, with this kind of technology won't be able to protect all this that should be the pride of the whole world?" asked Mary.

"You really think that all people are good and that they want to show a civilization more advanced than themselves, to show their weakness that they can't achieve anything new either in science or in art?", waving his hand, Dem constantly watched the city. Mary once again tried to get him to give a concrete answer: "But what will really happen to the city of pyramids?"

Dem took a few more steps, then suddenly turned around: "What's going to happen, what?", he uttered this somewhat his-singly, sighing deeply.

"My time is passing, we will try to return to our planet Tetran." If we succeed, we'll leave everything intact," he accompanied this sentence with a look at the sky as if he was seeing the constellation from which they had arrived.

"Now you see the splendor of greenery, noble and fruitful fields and abundance of water, and all that will one day be different." It will be a desert here and everything will be covered with sand, huuu, but everything," said Dem wistfully. Mary only now realized what it was that she had been missing all this time, even though she knew that in this place in the civilization where she lives, there is really a bare desert and only sand. For her, everything she had seen so far was enchanting, so she overlooked this fact. The magic of dream or reality - who knows what it really is, mostly continued, whether we wanted it or not. The multiplicity of events made the time immeasurable, so night was fast approaching. Mary and Dem stood motionless, transfixed by the imaginary scene. The sun was setting, casting a reddish light directly on the pyramids, and they were like the main actresses on the stage, with clean and sharp contours in a kind of haze of the setting sun. It's as if they're floating and as if someone dropped them right there, so it seems that they don't belong in that space, and on the other hand, they look like they've merged with the environment, which seems unimaginable without them.

Mary and Dem saw off the last ray that fell on the pyramids, and at the same time they sighed from the beauty of the scene. Dem invited Mary to go towards the city, and he put his palm to his face and said something to it. Swarms of lights soon appeared from the direction of the city, moving in irregular groupings. A moment later, Mary, surprised for the umpteenth time, notes that these swarms of light were swarms of golden bees. They were made of the purest gold and shone as if they had built-in glittering light bulbs. Well, those and such buzzing bees soon kept Dem and Mary company. Mary, mesmerized by this kind of accompaniment, extended her hand towards the bees to touch them, and they did not try to avoid the touch. Even one dares to land on Mary's face.

"Little madwoman, what are you doing here, so you don't bite me?", trying to touch her lightly with her hand, Mary felt something unrepeatable. The rapid beat of the bee's wings made a soft hum that tickled Mary's palm.

"Ha, ha, ha..." Mary laughed, offering her palm to Dem to see how she had made a new friend.

"I see, your hand is good and gentle, as you are a good human being yourself." "Many animals you will meet will not be able to resist you," Dem finished somewhat proudly. A scene beyond belief: two beings standing and sharing a moment of truth, thousands of years apart. The impossibility of explanation is aroused by desire like a flash in the eye. Soon the carriage appeared, which Mary had already had the opportunity to see, but now it came for her and Dem. They soon settled in it and set off, with bees above and around them lighting their way. A beautiful picture for fans of fairy-tale scenes that offered a completely different dimension.

In such pictures, one could always find everything beautiful that the viewer could wish for. The horses gently carried the carriage towards the city, and Mary could not resist expressing her thoughts aloud: "Me in a carriage made of gold, in another dimension, the civilization that I love the most throughout history!" I can't help but feel like a princess! What do you say?", she asked, knowing that he would get a wise answer. And she was not mistaken. "It is your right to feel that way." But, speaking of it, one does not have to have wealth to be a prince or princess, knowledge is wealth", Dem paused for a while, searching for the right words.

"When you have knowledge, then you are not a prince but a king!", he stopped talking, and pointed to the sky above the city, which was filled with fireworks as a sign of welcome for their guest. In different colors the sky was written: WELCOME, MARY, constantly showering the sky again and again with glittering dust. Although delighted, Mary managed to make out a quiet but steady song from the loud bursts of fireworks:

Welcome night, calm with sleep tight
I want a moon to move my bed
Star, show me the way instead
Take me into your lap
Do not give oblivion map
Take me on the right way
I want my life in old house, hey
I am tormented years and years
Dem, is it time to go without fears
This life does not match with the one that cheers.

Mary thought about the impression that this sad and wistful song left on her. It reflected the long-term suffering of these people who arrived on planet Earth against their will. Not giving her time to comment, Dem once again tried to explain to Mary their efforts to return to their home planet.

"Well, like every society, we also have problems with getting our compatriots used to this planet. After the exile from Tetran, with the help of Zakom, we sent the exact coordinates of the planet Earth, so many inhabitants soon came to it in their ships". There was a special warmth in Dem's voice.

"By the way, planet Earth was ideal for settlement after the ice age," Dem said, looking significantly at Mary. These were all like blows coming at regular intervals one after the other. Unpreparedness for this kind of knowledge took the last atom of strength out of Mary.

"What planet did we come from," she thought, looking at the color of her skin, though she never liked to think of diversity that way. Dem's ability to read minds prompts him to answer again.

"These are normal conclusions that are not and should not be a burden to you. Every realization, if it is correct, should awaken in you a new energy for an explanation, because without it every event loses its meaning", Dem shifted in his seat, looking for a more comfortable position.

An avalanche of questions started again in Mary. "Why are we in a carriage as a means of transportation in addition to advanced technologies and is it so ideal on this planet that your people are bored and want to return to Tetran?" Mary snapped impatiently.

"Easy, easy, not so ideal. Through the carriage, you should understand what tradition is and how it is preserved. Even though I could cover distances in an hour with the help of laser technology, I decided to use a carriage for receptions and the arrival of dear guests", he proudly notes to Mary what a tradition it is.

"We do have problems. Requests to return to Tetran are not the only problem we have. There is one much worse", he said at the end of the sentence somewhat quietly, as if he was afraid that someone would hear him. Mary looked at him in astonishment, not believing that people like this could have problems.

"May I know what the problem is, Dem, what's got you so scared?", Mary finished matter-of-factually, as if she possessed unlimited powers.

Steel birds riders

All flustered, Dem put a finger to his mouth gesturing to Mary to talk quietly. The bees were still shining their light on the carriage that was driving towards the city, and the first streets were already getting closer. Mary felt a strange kind of fear, like that primal fear you feel, but you don't know its origin.

A slight shiver went through her whole body. She wanted them to come to the palace as soon as possible. A strong stream of light suddenly appeared from the sky, which in an instant wiped out the bees and created complete darkness.

"What's this, Dem, did someone turn off the electricity?", she tried to joke.

"It's impossible!" cried Dem. "The worst premonitions seem to be coming true!" No, that can't be!", said Dem in an almost panicked voice. Not long after that, Dem opened the screen between his hands and issued a few commands.

"Agans, activate the protective roof over the city, reduce the use of light to a minimum." Send a sailboat for me and Mary now!"

Unlike a while ago, Dem was the real ruler who knows what to do even in the most difficult moments.

Soon an automated glider arrives, without a pilot. "Who's going to fly this craft?" Mary asked. Dem touched her, and signaled her to come in and don't waste much time.

Soon, Mary realized that this craft also works with thought commands. They set off, but again towards the pyramids.

"I have to hide you there." The conquerors of the system are coming and you must not disappear, because the entire civilization that follows would perish", the moment he uttered this, they were already in front of the pyramids. The door of the craft opened silently. Again, Dem gestured to her to follow him.

And just as the door began to open, something fell at their feet. Dem moved his hand in that direction. His hand glowed and illuminated a bag that read, "Delivery for Mary, Urgent." She was startled by what she saw. What shipment at this time and in this place? Dem was already untying the sack from which, to Mary, already familiar head appeared. It was Neci: "Was someone looking for me by any chance?", he said mischievously in a way that only he can. Nothing was clear to Dem anymore. "Now who is this and what is he doing here, at this very time when the Steelbird Riders are about to attack us, a nightmare for anyone who meets them?"»

"You just take us to the pyramid, this is my cousin." I don't know either where he came from, but we'll talk about that later", Mary hurriedly said this, and headed towards the door, which was now wide open.

Soon they entered and heard the door close. The interior was lit by a bright yellow light. Dem grabbed safety glasses from the shelf and handed them to Mary and Neci. Due to the strength of the light, they could not see the corridors or the direction they should go. However, when they have put on the glasses, everything changed.

The glasses themselves, in addition to protection from light, offered a number of other possibilities, such as a road map, a direction for a safe exit and the possibility of using a concealing veil.

If they encountered an opponent, it was enough to activate this veil that would cover the person and make them invisible. A series of corridors that branched off on all four sides offered interesting drawings, as well as letters known as hieroglyphics. The perfection of the script and the perfection of the colors gave the appearance of a film carved in granite stone.

They couldn't stay long in front of this scene, they had to follow Dem who was hurrying towards the central part of the pyramid. A big yellow circle on black granite, on which the stars were arranged, greeted them in the central part of the pyramid. Dem stood next to it and began to wave lightly over the circle. Soon, both the circle and the stars simply came off the granite and took their place at the height of Dem's head.

The stars pulsated and danced as if they were dancing to the rhythm of the music, while some would bulge out, others would retract and everything would be in perfect order.

"'What you see is the constellation R.S.N.P. - 2007. We as a civilization come from this planet,'" Dem said, pointing to the one closest to the center, taking it and pulling it out of the hovering circle.

He shook it a little and it became the size of a basketball. Now the relief of the planet, mountains, rivers, larger cities and dozens of pyramids were already visible.

What was strangest of all was the color of the planet. It was the color of gold.

"This really is gold. My planet Tetran is 40% made of gold, and the larger percentage, of 60%, is water, which gives the balance of life on the planet", it seemed as if he was in a terrible hurry to say something very important to Mary, and now also to the newcomer Neci.

"'We, as the ruling family, were actually banished

from Tetran,'" continued Dem, caressing the planet gently. "We found this planet we were sent to never reach, but thanks to Kazum, we did find it. And you, Mary, saw what we managed to build."

"Yes, you are right, you are Dem. What I saw exceeds all the expectations of even the greatest dreamers"," Mary supported him expecting the main part of Dem's story.

"To simplify, upon arriving on planet Earth we started with the realization of only one idea - to build powerful ships to return to Tetran and overthrow the black rule of Olz who, with the help of the ruler of darkness whose name should not be spoken, conquered half of the Pulsar constellation, while advancing towards other solar systems", he was still playing with the planet, moving it from hand to hand.

"This pyramid in which we are now is actually a powerful ship, which has another one below it only facing downwards"" while talking, Dem closely followed the expressions on the faces of Neci and Mary.

Mary, all impatient, already in the fire of questions, speeds up: "» So, this upside-down pyramid of the same dimensions is below us. Why?"

"On our planet Tetran, all the ships, even the palaces, look like pyramids. The ships were planned that way because they were the easiest to fill with energy, and the pyramid, due to the structure of the sides, provides the answer to countless mathematical puzzles".

Dem pulled his hands from top to bottom, and a large screen appeared. An image of outer space appeared, but not the one we know from the movies - this was much more restless and dangerous. Large fleets of ships were already close to the solar system in which the planet Earth is, according to what the direction and distance showed.

Mary went to stop this force of ships with her hand, and then realized that it was just a picture, and turned to Dem: "What's going on?" It looks like this is an invasion of our planet. Neci, help us prevent this!", Mary squeezed Neci's hand.

"No, no! Mary, there's no need to panic., What you saw is really close, but they haven't yet received an official report from the Steel Bird Riders about my presence here. Nothing matters to them but me, they want me", Dem said coldly despite the impending danger.

He went into the room next to this one, which was spacious and lit with milky white light.

Without a lot of elements, only with a flashing control desk, while in the central part, there were sunbeds made of gold in the shape of a human body that offer the possibility of being closed with a lid of the same shape, of course, everything was made of pure gold.

"These are our lounge chairs for travel. After programming the route, we would lie down in deck-chairs where we would fall into a deep sleep, and everything is controlled by the central computer",» - Dem pointed to the glass column through which balls in all possible colors were constantly moving.

"This is futile, even though you have an extremely developed civilization. So do you think that computers are infallible, that they can't put you in a kind of danger, right?", said Mary angrily, realizing all the powerlessness of man and technology.

Dem thought about these words. They shook him deeply because finally, someone confirmed what he had suspected for years, that the events and premonitions to come would not be prevented by anything, not even such strong technology that they possess. He ran his hand across the screen and Metal Bird Riders appeared, more machines than living beings. They rode huge birds like the drag-

ons of the stories, only these were made of metal. We'll call them Metal Dragon Riders because birds are fine creatures. So, these metal dragons with big and staring eyes that turned in all directions, gave the Riders all the important information related to navigation and destinations such as the proximity of the desired target. The Riders themselves were a separate story; they were provided with equipment just like the old knights, made of a combination of precious metals so that they provided a kind of protection against any kind of weapon.

And they themselves managed the dragons with metal reins on the principle of riding a horse. As weapons, they had great fast nets that, when they discovered the chased, they would throw and hunt with 100% hunting efficiency. We should also mention the logo-top that they used before casting the net. By including them, they would erase the use of logic by the persecuted.

Therefore, such an opponent had to be tackled. The fight was uncertain from the very beginning.

"And what will happen to your family, they are the closest to you? Isn't there a danger that they will be taken away too?", Mary asked, worrying about Adan and Argi. "Oooohhh", Dem sighed heavily, bowed his head and at that moment two tears rolled down his cheeks.

They jingled like coins as they fell on the granite. Neci came up to him and grabbed him under the arm for a moment of silence.

"It is true my child that your meeting with my son and daughter is indeed nothing short of reality, but it has been two years since they and my wife were taken away by the Steel Dragon Riders.

All I have is a four-dimensional projection that somehow makes up for their absence.", he couldn't stand it anymore and started crying again. Mary also cried, she was very touched by the feeling of losing those closest to her. She approached Dema and she hugged him. It meant a lot to him, and after a few moments, as he collected himself, he began to think about what to do.

He asked the computer for weapon options for defense, as well as tactics that would be best suited to counter the Riders.

Life-size uniforms and weapons to fight against the Riders began to be projected.

A A - A vest covered in net-cutting blades, and a cough spray.

B - Hat and gloves with flamethrowers, and duck feathers for tickling.

C - Backpack with jet engines, water gun.

D - Large soap bubble ejector, graffiti spray.

E -- Liquid permanent glue, and fan with mechanical arms for slapping.

F - The best food and the fastest in unlimited quantities, anti-appetite syrup.

G - Music that makes you want to dance whether you like it or not, a speed booster to unimaginable limits.

H - Wand with various spells, instructions for non-use.

I - Modulator for changing languages, e.g. Chinese, spray for unlimited laughter.

J - A story for the late night that turns bad people into good people, sneakers for non-stop running

It was the first of the uniform models with additional equipment. Although the situation was tense, seeing this, Neci burst out laughing. Dem watched him, but nothing was clear to him.

"Why is he laughing?" Dem asked Mary.

"You need to understand that in our time the wars that are being fought use far more deadly weapons that cause far worse consequences. These are your children's toys compared to that", and Mary replied to Dem with a smile.

Dem accepted this with disbelief, and explained.

"Look, these invaders, i.e. Riders do not use weapons for destruction, only for capture. According to the galactic convention, no weapon that can threaten any form of life may be used," said Dem angrily.

"All this that happened and half the constellation was conquered, it's all because that convention is being violated! They also use deadly weapons! I must empha-

size here that those who use such weapons after leaving this world, the Creator turns into infinite nothingness." Dem fell silent after what he said, expecting the reactions of Mary and Neci, who in the meantime had stopped laughing. Mary started nervously pacing the room, looking for the meaning of all this. She suddenly thought of an idea and hastened to announce it: "Let Neci and I put on our uniforms, take these weapons, and fight with Riders, what do you think, Dem?"

He jumped: "No, no! No way! I told you that the development of civilizations would take a completely different course", he said nervously, and somehow scared.

"So who will, if I may ask?" According to you, that should be an army that does not exist, and which was a projection. You only have Agans and a few other workers who were exiled from Tetran with you, right? Even the city is a fictional image from your planet. You played with our feelings!", she was also referring to Neci, even though he didn't see anything. Dem was surprised by Mary's thinking. It was clear to him that it was not without reason that she was chosen to return from her world to this ancient civilization.

"I'm really surprised, you quickly found out what it was about!" Everything was a projection that you, as a good medium, accepted. Only the pyramid is real, with all the listed possibilities," said Dem, red in the face.

Neci was already rummaging through the designed equipment and weapons, while his hand was swiping quickly the pictorial instructions. And whoop, Mary and Neci were already dressed in uniforms with all the necessary weapons in the next moment. They looked at each other and smiled, looking surprisingly ordinary to each other, as if they had been in this outfit for years.

"We're sorry, Dem, that we have to do some things that you didn't approve of, but life doesn't choose its participants," Mary said this so fiercely that she didn't give any room for Dem's counter-orders.

Mary looked at her watch: it was exactly five minutes past midnight. Maybe enough, maybe a little time for the decisive battle with the Riders.

"I think it's time to take a nap then with the first rays of the sun into the fight!", concluded Mary, thinking of a comfortable deckchair that immediately found itself in the room just as she had imagined.

Neci and Dem realized that there was nothing to discuss further, so they did the same.

The flickering and dim light cast a glare on the three sleeping persons, who at this moment are each dreaming their own dream.

What's going on outside? We should also take a look there. The sky was clear and sprinkled with stars, and it wasn't so dark on the ground.

About fifty meters from the pyramid was the camp of the Steel Dragon Riders. They were gathered around the swarm of bees that they had taken from

Dem last night, debating whether to report the location to Big Olz right away or wait until morning to catch Dem, of which they were sure.

They knew that for such news, Olz was giving away great treasures, as well as functions that guaranteed a safe and comfortable life. The superior among them laughed. His laugh was more like a horse's neigh than a human laugh. After that, he spoke in a hoarse voice: "I swear to you, there's no need to report now, it's better to do it when we're done with Dem!" It will bring us more glory and wealth", he said this while turning around and looking at the faces of his soldiers. They were silent, which could only mean unquestioning obedience.

"Let's sing the song of the victors," he roared so loudly that the entire valley echoed and even the steel dragons were disturbed.-

I am strong that I can not be more
Be nice- what is that meaning for?
We have a flying dragons you see
And the future kings to be
Evil is our stronger side
Good from us must go and hide
Who comes on our way
Will not wait for a next day.
Darkness is our best pal
In that circle evil comes as well
We have never lost any fight
We make evil every day and night.

The song ends with choral singing. After that, he issued an order for rest and a duty to keep watch. Soon, the outside world became silent, the bees turned off the lights, and they fell asleep as well. Everything was sleeping: the night, the moon, the stars, evil and good, both those outside and those inside the pyramid.

So when everything sleeps, does this story sleep? No – it does not, it moves on.

What will happen tomorrow, who will win? The constant struggle between good and evil continues. Mary had been dreaming for a long time now. Although the dream was turbulent, she kept quite calm.

At one point Neci jumped making movements like when two opponents are fighting, then when he quickly resolved the fight, of course, in his favor, he lay down again as if nothing had happened.

The pendulum of the clock worked incessantly tick-tock, tick-tock, tick-tock, the time of decision was approaching.

Was there fear in any of the participants in this fight? Hey, that's a real question! There is no hero whose heart did not beat faster, not from nervousness but from fear.

Whoever tells you that he was never scared, know this: He is not telling the truth.

The sun covered the pyramid and the area around it with its rays, the Riders began to wake up, as well as the guard who was supposed to be awake all night.

And the interior of the pyramid soon came to life. Mary was already brushing her teeth, Neci was washing, and Dem, who had already done so, was scrolling through the floating screen looking for more information about the Steel Dragon Riders. Mary spoke up: "Take a closer look at what these guys are doing outside and how we can get out without being jumped right away," she looked straight at Dem.

Dem turned on the outer segment and, to Mary's and Neci's astonishment, the independent galactic media had already informed their consumers that there were now hundreds of crews out there ready to film what was billed as the fight of all fights. This is the struggle that decides the further existence and development of civilization. It is known: If good wins, there will be light, and if evil wins, there will be darkness.

Mary instantly realized that this turn of events was good for them - at least they would have the support of an independent audience across the galaxies who would be doing the broadcasts. She just waved to Neci, and they started moving towards the exit. Dem simply didn't find a way to stop them and they just pressed the mechanism to open the door.

Mary turned to him once more: "Don't leave the

pyramid under any circumstances until we finish the job," she said as if this was some trickery, not a decisive battle. When they got outside the pyramid, they were greeted by journalists dressed in white suits with the names of the agencies they report for.

There was a general commotion. Everyone asked the same questions in unison as to what they expected from the fight and whether they would be able to win. They told them, among other things, that the bookies said they had no chance of winning. Already walking through the crowd, Mary briefly answered the question about the winner.

"If the Riders knew what awaited them, they would have disappeared from this galaxy a long time ago, and let the bookies do their dirty work." Whoever invests in us will become a billionaire." The stadium designed for that occasion was already expecting Mary and Neci.

Accompanied by two well-trained ushers, they arrived at the stadium, which was filled to capacity. As they stepped into it, they were overwhelmed by the noise and shouts of the onlookers who were cheering for these two weak fighters against the seven Steel Dragon Riders. Mary raised her hand and there was silence in the stadium. A microphone also appeared out of nowhere.

"Greetings! I want to sing you a little song before the fight starts", Mary bowed and began:

A TRUTH SONG

In front of us you stand there
For your lives salvation will be somewhere
The space is truth for all of us
One voice gives orders and discuss
That one that pushes in the night
Should realize it is not on a sight
The truth is the one that breaks
It is a shame that all good takes
Like all of you are just insane
The fight must started all again.
Powerful fighters you will meet
Behind me is light, behind you a night sweet
I promise, alone I will gain a battle complete.

Neci glanced towards Mary, not believing what he had just heard, and thinking that it must be a reaction out of fear. Opposite them stood the Riders, still not mounted on the dragons. That desire, and at the same time their inability to resist, brought countless people from unknown planets whose names you couldn't even pronounce.

Mary took a close look at the Riders who were veritable scions of evil, greased and disheveled as they held their metal headgear in their hands and glared at their opponents. The commander signaled with his hand to prepare for battle, and the entire stadium fell silent. The cry of the drag-on seemed to mark the beginning of the fight: "Gggvvvvviiiiii", the announcement sounded like the loudest squeal, and the ears almost could not endure this volume.

As if on command, the eight of them rode the dragons, and surrounded Neci and Mary in silence. A natural reaction ensued between the two. In an instant they were leaning back to back, so they had a view of all the Riders.

The first net took off towards Mary and Netius. A loud whistle followed her flight and what's more interesting, as she got closer to her target, she got bigger and bigger.

Mary quickly said, "Get into the hedgehog pose, put your feet and hands down on the ground, and your back as high as possible in the air, quickly!" They both immediately got into that pose as quickly as if they had been practicing for days. The net was already falling on them, but without effect, on the backs of Mary and Neci, there were sharp blades that cut the net. This sight caused a sigh of admiration from the audience, while it caused disbelief from the Riders. Mary went on the offensive, turning on the fan with outstretched slapping arms, the two closest Riders being kicked out of their dragon saddles. At that moment, Neci spilled quick-setting glue under the feet of the dragons, who ran straight into it. The howls of helplessness from these animals that could not move filled the stadium.

They arched their necks and widened their eyes even more with the horrible screeching of the metal they were made of. "Let's finish off these two dragons," Neci stated and turned on the jet pack taking out the water gun. In the next few moments, no one could see Neci, he was very quick with flying around the dragons, and all this was accompanied by flooding the dragon's most vital parts with water.

With a sound like a car braking at high speed, Neci stood next to Mary. The smile never left her face. She hadn't expected this in her wildest dreams, but they had already eliminated two dragons, and without them, the Riders were like turtles without shells.

Dem watched the fight with great anxiety, but these first moments cheered him up, there was hope for a favorable outcome that could result in the release of his loved ones.

The commander of the Riders now received an order from Olz: "You must win this fight, use secret weapons, they must not survive!" Be careful, if by any chance they win, you know what awaits you as a reward from me, ha, ha, ha", echoed a creepy laugh in the Rider's headphones. The commander stepped forward in front of his Riders, and as in American football, he began to show using his fingers behind his back the combination that his soldiers should take as the only possible and winning one.

The Riders set off even more decisively, the dragons were already spewing fire, and lasers appeared in the hands of the soldiers. Out of surprise, the auditorium also made noise; this was turning into a dangerous fight in which lives were at risk. Neci winked at Mary and played music that you couldn't resist. The dragons began a sort of kan-kan dance throwing their legs into the air, not leaving the Riders who flew out of their saddles.

As they fell, they jumped to their feet and began to dance. Neci approached one by one and handed out sneakers.

They accepted them with enthusiasm, and quickly put on their sneakers. Whit Riders, the old saying proved right: Just let it be for free, at least. The sneakers were tip-top, and the Riders stared at them from every side. It was only for a moment because soon the sneakers started to do their job. There was such a race that it was not known who was chasing whom and who was currently first, and what was the purpose of their running. They were trying to stop, creating a very funny sight. The upper part of the body was somehow tilted backward to the legs. The stadium was shaking with laughter, the galaxy was also shaking, they hadn't seen a funnier sight in a long time.

This would probably go on forever if a very icy wind did not blow on these runners. As the temperature dropped, so did the runners, until they froze and stood in strange positions like ice sculptures.

Meri and Neci looked at each other. "What happened now, huh?" Mary asked. This did not last for long, the stadium and spectators disappeared, the reporters disappeared, and only the sky was written like neon: "Disturbances in broadcasting." The sky also darkened, a cold wind blew, and then Olz appeared, an evil that could be smelled and felt because it was so strong. He thundered in a blood-chilling voice:

"You little nothingness, shadows of nothingness, you dare to oppose the prince of darkness! Who are you and what galaxy do you come from? Bow down if you want my mercy!" Although he looked dark as evil, being wrapped in the blackest cloak the two of them had ever seen, they didn't let him see fear on their faces. Mary mustered up her courage and addressed Olz:

You fight against the light
Concur galaxies without mercy tight
You wish for a darkness lord
You will get only graves and sword.
The good for you is a painful wound
For empire you do not need much round
I am not scare at all of death
In a battle with me you will lose breath
The master can be just one
But you are not valuable, son
Prepare yourself for a final fight
You will lose on day or night.

The origin of the planet Earth seems to be the reason for the constant friction and struggle between good and evil. And now, here, in this place in the shadow of the pyramids, a fight was to take place that would most likely change the course of history. Meri was shaking with fear and couldn't even swallow because her throat was tight. She looked at Neci. With protruding eyes, his gaze fixed on Olz, no doubt that he didn't feel better than Mary either.

Just the right helper

The sun was shining warmly even though it was gradually getting older outside. Mary realized that the coldness was coming from Olz, who was still standing there staring at them. Mary heard a voice behind her: "Don't worry, you and Neci just move aside for this fight." a familiar voice finished. Meri and Neci, as if on command, moved to the side to let that brave fighter pass who, as it seemed, was not afraid of Olz.

A man wrapped in a white cloak interwoven with golden beads passed by, bringing with him the warmth of the sun again. Mary recognized him: it was the stranger from the plane, or, as Adan and Argy said, the Time Keeper.
Olz kind of recoiled when he saw him. "You can't take part in this, I hope you understand!" thundered Olz in a panic.
"Hahaha! You can't order me around! Who are you? Who? The most ordinary nothing! You are like some kind of horror from evil! Am I right, tell me!?" said the Time Keeper approaching Olz.

At that moment Olz began:

Storms, winds, rain I beg you with all bad
Come with me in the fight mad
To get rid of this pain
Let him know who is the boss main
I see you are defending your blood
Your days are finished like ground in flood
And you do not have so much luck
Bigger opponents in a defeat stuck.

He turned his hands towards the Keeper of Time and started pelting him with lightning bolts and balls of thunder, but the Keeper didn't even move. They could very well hear him laughing: "Don't, please! You're tickling me, ha, ha, ha." He immediately stopped laughing and lowered his cloak, then said straight to Olz: "I don't need lightning or thunder! With these hands, I will finish with you", suddenly the hands grew, and they pushed Olz.
What followed cannot even be described. Olz, the embodiment of evil that gave him strength, began to cry and beg for mercy.
"Let me go, please! I won't say anything to little Mary. You are known for the fact that you wouldn't

even step on an ant, and look what you are doing to me!", now his voice turned into a sob. Mary didn't miss what Olz said to the Time Keeper about her.

She turned to Neci: "Did you hear what that ugly thing said?", she demanded an answer.

And Neci had wondered off ever since the Guardian of Time stepped onto the battlefield, especially when he heard his voice. He was flooded with memories of when he was three or four years old, actually from the time when he could remember. That voice was something that took him back to his childhood. Trying to figure out his past brought him to the verge of tears.

During that time, Mary tried to make him listen, which she eventually succeeded in doing.

Whaaat...What's up Mary?", he answered as if he had just gotten out of bed.

"What happened to you, man, where have you wandered off to?" I asked you, did you hear what this Olz said, something related to me?", she looked at Neci, and saw tears in his eyes. "What's wrong with you, why are you crying? Answer me!", she began to shake him, and she cried too. Tears rolled down like rivers, pearls of tears spilled onto the ground, soaking it. The Time Keeper had overpowered Olz, so he was now watching these two young people cry. He himself remembered his own tears, realizing that they are often an eraser of sadness or proof of joy. He knew very well the reason for the crying of Mary and Neci. They understood who he was. He had very little time left to spend with these two brave young people. He opened his mouth to call to Mary, but no voice came out. He tried to signal

them with his hand to come closer, but his hand didn't listen to him either. He cried like he had never cried before. All three were sobbing, bursting into tears.

Tears were their only way of communication, questions were asked through tears and answers came through tears. The strongest communication in the world is when we are born. And then we begin the story with the outside world with tears.

When we leave this world, those who love us cry for us. Dem also watched this story told with tears on his screen. He could not stand it, so he came out of the pyramid and hugged Mary and Neci.

The Time Keeper was slowly melting like snow in the spring sun. His contours became fainter and fainter until they disappeared completely

The return

Olz was lying on the ground bound and blindfolded. That was important for him if he was to be prevented from dirty and evil intentions. Dem moved aside, asking Neci and Mary not to look towards Olz. They obeyed him, still wiping away tears.
Dem approached Olz and whispered in his ear that if he wanted to live, he should urgently write the code for the release of his loved ones.

Olz did not think twice and gave him a sign that he accepted. Dem untied one of his hands and gave him a paper and a pen. Although he only had one hand free, Olz quickly typed the code, expecting a quick release. The sky stirred and dark clouds began to fly. A heavy rain breaks and a strong wind blows out of nowhere, and as suddenly as it began, it ended as well. Dem's loved ones appeared - wife Anitsi leading Argi and Adana, and Kazom was behind them on all fours.
Mary and Neci watched the joy of the family reunion. They did not envy them because they too were at least for a short time with the

person they loved very much. Dem embraced his family and called Mary and Neci, who joined him in rejoicing. They entered the pyramid, and transported the wicked Olz to an uninhabited planet in the JARK constellation, and continued with rejoicing and curious questions from both sides. "Mary, you've seen everything you should have seen." I hope you're not mad at me for showing some flaws that confirm that there are no perfect people but one should try to be honest and fair in all of this," he said sadly, knowing that the end of this friendship was coming.

"I have one more request for you and Neci: Since the pyramid is built, you should help us with just one more thing, please."

"Just say it, Dem, it will be an honor for us to help such an honorable man once again," said Mary, overjoyed to be able to do something for Dem. They entered the central room where there were deckchairs in the shape of their bodies and took their seats. From his prone position, Dem said to Mary, "Now just close the trunks, and when you close them before you go out, press the red button on the main computer. After that, you have twenty seconds to leave the ship," said Dem decisively, hiding his sadness at parting with these two wonderful young people.

"But how are you going to take off?" Is everything all right?" Mary sped up.

"Everything is planned perfectly! We are return-

ing to our home planet, and good luck to you, as a reward I will leave you with knowledge about this that will not be erased from your memory. Just take it easy in your time and carefully in using that knowledge!"

All three put their hands over their hands with open palms towards their shoulders. Meri and Neci began to close the coffins, ran their hands over the exquisitely made reliefs of beautiful letters and unique pictures. They were about to leave towards the computer when they saw Kazom curled up next to the coffin. "What are you doing here, are you going to travel like that without a suitcase?" ", Mary and Neci asked him in unison. He did not answer them, only two tears rolled down his beautiful face and clattered on the granite. Neci pulled Mary by the sleeve: "Let's go, it's time", continuing to drag her to the control panel, and, as if on command, they pressed the red button together. In an instant he felt a slight tremor; the engines started, and the two were moving quickly towards the exit.

Happy and exited, they moved a decent distance away to watch the strangely shaped ship take off: A flying pyramid, imagine that!

But nothing of the expected happened but something that they could not even dream of.

Kazom jumped out of the pyramid in one big jump through its granite walls, landed on all fours, then made another jump towards the valley below the pyramid. Neci and Mary witnessed a real miracle. While still in the air, Kazom grew in size and increased by a hundred times so that when he landed in the valley he was in the position of a lying lion and a human head looking somewhere far away like a guardian. As the transformation of a living organism into a petrified sculpture came to an end, Neci and Mary looked at the pyramid. An even greater miracle occurred when a transparent glass smaller pyramid emerged from that pyramid and flew into the sky.

"What just happened Neci?" Mary asked.

Neci, confused himself, muttered, "This is like in the movies when the soul leaves the body."
For just a moment, they saw a transparent pyramid, which soon disappeared.
"Let's go on, children! What we see in the valley of the pyramid is the famous sphinx - half lion and half man, which is the guardian of Khafre's pyramid. Neci and

Mary, you've wandered off somewhere again, please pay attention!", class teacher Melika continued to explain the history of Egypt. Mary and Neci stared at each other. They could not understand anything.
And you? Could you understand anything in this story?

THE END

WEIRD GUESTS

Author: **Fahrudin Kučuk**

Publisher: Globland Books
London, 2024.

Translator: **Dragana Pavlović Ribać**

Designer / Illustrator : **Enesa Ustamujić-Sejdić**